Thunder and the Noise Storms

Words by
Jeffrey Ansloos and Shezza Ansloos

Pictures by
Joshua Mangeshig Pawis-Steckley

annick
press
toronto · berkeley

Noise storms at school are the worst.

On Monday there was a big storm. It started on the bus, with all the kids laughing and waving at the cars driving past, trying to get them to honk their horns.

Honk, honk, honk!

I got that funny feeling in my body and my brain felt woozy.

At school, everyone was talking, and all the jackets, shoes, and backpacks scraped and swished as the other kids put them in their cubbies.

All that racket made me grumpy.

In music class on Tuesday, my friends were singing at the top of their lungs. When the teacher said we could use the instruments, my head felt like it would explode.

I pulled up my hoodie so I could be by myself.

Gym class on Wednesday was rough.

Sneakers squeaking, the teacher blowing the whistle, and the balls bouncing.

Boom, boom, boom!

I couldn't stay there one more second. I was so mad, I kicked the ball as hard as I could. It hit the bench and knocked over all the water bottles.

Recess was even tougher.

When the bell rang and the kids ran
to line up, someone bumped me.
I yelled at everyone to leave me alone.
The kids backed away and stared.

The principal called my mosom to come help. By the time Mosom got there, I was crying and embarrassed.

Mosom said, "When you're ready, Thunder, you can come down. I'll just wait here."

It got quiet when everyone went back into the school. I climbed down, and at the bottom of the slide, Mosom was waiting.

He smiled and said,
"Let's go for a walk."

I love walks with Mosom.

After a while he asked, "Thunder, why were you hiding?"

I told him that sometimes things get too noisy. It's just so loud and I can't stand it.

Mosom nodded. "It's like that for me too, sometimes."

He explained that when he was a little boy, his father taught him a special word to help him with noise storms.

The word is mamaskasitawew.
It means to listen with wonder.

Mosom said, "Sometimes life is noisy, and sometimes life is wonderful . . .
especially when you listen to the quiet things. There is wonder all around us."

I tried to listen to the quiet things Mosom spoke about, but I didn't hear anything.

I still felt stormy. My face was hot, and my skin felt scratchy.
All I heard was the swing set, screeching in the breeze.

Mosom closed his eyes, then he said,
"Thunder, Thunder, listen with wonder. Can you hear our
relative the wind? The wind is singing a soothing song."

I stopped to listen again. It was hard at first.
I only heard annoying songs. The flag whipping,
a door banging, and the gravel grinding under my feet.

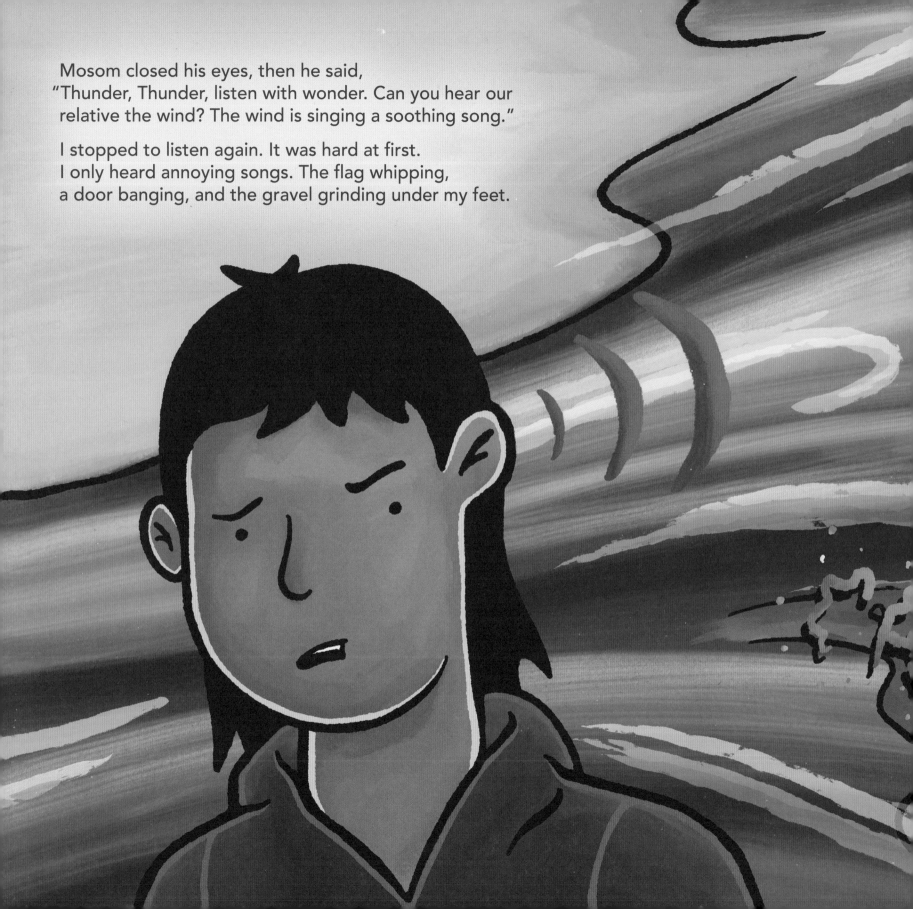

I closed my eyes, and then I heard it.

Whoooooooooosh, whoooooooooosh, whoooooooooosh.

The windsong made me happy.
I could feel the song on my skin.

Mosom looked around. "Can you hear the trees? Listen closely."

The branches moved slowly. I could hear them creak and sway. I could hear the leaves too. They were clapping and giving each other high fives. I giggled.

"What about the squirrels, Thunder?"

I listened closely, just like Mosom. I heard them talking to us.
I thought they said hello.

Mosom waved at the squirrels and said, "Tanisi, little friends."
Then he pointed to the sky. "Listen to the birds fly."

I heard their wings, flapping and swooping.
Mosom asked if I could hear their strength.
As I watched them move in the sky, I felt stronger.

Mosom looked towards the river and said, "Sometimes the waters are loud, but today the river is quiet. I wonder what the river is saying?"

I paused to listen and thought that maybe the river was saying to slow down. I asked Mosom if we could walk a little slower.

"Yes, Thunder, that's a good idea," he said.

SPLASH

BURBL

"Can you hear the sweetgrass whispers?" Mosom asked.

I heard them say that there's a lot going on, but everything was going to be okay. I wondered if Mosom heard them too.

Mosom said, "There is a lot going on, Thunder, but we can face it together."

"Let's just stand here, quiet and still," Mosom said. "Do you hear it?"

At first, I noticed the cars rumbling past. A siren screamed and a big dog barked. My body got stiff and I squeezed my hands.

Mosom said, "Let's take some deep breaths."
Mosom breathed in and out. The sound made me feel better.

Mosom asked to hold my hand. I said yes.
Then I heard it. It sounded like a drum. A slow and steady drum.

Badoom, badoom, badoom.

"What's that?" I asked Mosom.

"That's your heart," he said. "What's your heart saying to you, Thunder?"

I listened. "I think it is saying there is wonder all around us, and inside us too."

Mosom smiled. "Let's just sit here," he said.

We sat listening to all the quiet sounds.

"Do you want to go back?" Mosom asked.

"Yes," I told him.

I felt ready. I was calm and the noise storm was gone.

We walked back to school and I joined my friends in class.

Today, there was a fire drill. It was a big noise storm.

The bells ringing, the kids getting up from their desks, the noisy walk to the safe spot outside, and the roll call. It was really, really, really loud.

I started to get that funny feeling again.

I took some deep breaths and listened for the quiet sounds. I remembered what Mosom said.

"Thunder, Thunder, listen with wonder."

Even with all the noise around me,
I could still listen to my heart.

For Matthew, Kîsik, and all the quiet things.
–J.A. and S.A.

In loving memory of Taran Kootenhayoo. Neghanighita.
–J.M.P-S.

Mosom is the Cree word for "grandpa."
Tanisi is the Cree word for "hello."

JEFFREY ANSLOOS is a Cree educator and psychologist, and the Canada Research Chair in Critical Studies in Indigenous Health and Social Action on Suicide. He is the author of *The Medicine of Peace: Indigenous Youth Decolonizing Healing and Resisting Violence*.

SHEZZA ANSLOOS is a Cree writer, educator, artist, and speaker. She is the author of two children's books, *I Loved Her* and *The Fire Walker*. Ansloos is also an award-winning singer-songwriter and visual artist.

JOSHUA MANGESHIG PAWIS-STECKLEY is an Anishinaabe artist/illustrator from Wasauksing First Nation. He is a self-taught artist who works in the Woodland art style of the Anishinaabe people.

© 2021 Jeffrey Ansloos and Shezza Ansloos (text)
© 2021 Joshua Mangeshig Pawis-Steckley (illustrations)
Second printing, December 2021

Cover art by Joshua Mangeshig Pawis-Steckley,
designed by Paul Covello
Interior designed by Paul Covello
Edited by Claire Caldwell

Annick Press Ltd.

We acknowledge the support of the Canada Council for the Arts and the Ontario Arts Council, and the participation of the Government of Canada/ la participation du gouvernement du Canada for our publishing activities.

ONTARIO ARTS COUNCIL
CONSEIL DES ARTS DE L'ONTARIO
an Ontario government agency
un organisme du gouvernement de l'Ontario

Library and Archives Canada Cataloguing in Publication

Title: Thunder and the noise storms / words by Jeffrey Ansloos and Shezza Ansloos ; pictures by Joshua Mangeshig Pawis-Steckley.
Names: Ansloos, Jeffrey Paul, author. | Ansloos, Shezza, author. | Pawis-Steckley, Joshua Mangeshig, illustrator.
Identifiers: Canadiana (print) 20210188804 | Canadiana (ebook) 20210188855 | ISBN 9781773215587 (hardcover) | ISBN 9781773215617 (PDF) | ISBN 9781773215600 (HTML)
Subjects: LCGFT: Picture books.
Classification: LCC PS8601.N548 T48 2021 | DDC jC813/.6—dc23

Published in the U.S.A. by Annick Press (U.S.) Ltd.
Distributed in Canada by University of Toronto Press.
Distributed in the U.S.A. by Publishers Group West.

Printed in China

annickpress.com
jeffreyansloos.com
shezzaansloos.com
joshuamangeshig.com

Also available as an e-book. Please visit annickpress.com/ebooks for more details.